Prickly Rose

Shelley Gill • *Illustrated by* Judy Love

ini Charlesbridge

Legend says the Rose girls
towered ten feet tall.
Truth is, Sitka did so;
Prickly, not at all.

When Sitka called her "squirt,"
not being a girl to whine,
Prickly simply bristled
like a porcupine.

Hearing Sitka's tales
of riding whales and hunting gold,
Prickly felt left out—
and that was getting old.

Heading north at break-up,
Sitka mushed toward Nome.
Prickly swore, "Not this time!
I won't be stuck at home!"

"Sitka, where'd you go?"
Prickly yelled o'er icy seas.
She jumped aboard two orcas
and learned to water-ski.

They hit Lituya Bay.
Prickly capsized—SPLASH!
She sparked a great tsunami
that hit the coastline—CRASH!

Once ashore she sniffed.
What was in the air?
Sitka's moldy toes?
No! A glacier bear!

Prickly hopped aboard,
and off the twosome flew,
joined by a wolf and ermine.
The porcupine came, too!

Nighttime tracking stunk
without the moon as guide,
so Prickly yanked it closer
and formed Alaska's tides.

When Prickly stomped o'er ridges,
Alaska got the shakes:
    spruce began to tremble;
    critters yelled, "Earthquake!"

Jumping peak to peak,
she tripped and fell below.
Prickly's temper boiled!
It made the mountain blow!

Crashing near Ophir,
Prickly saw a sign.
Peering close, she read it:
"Welcome to Anvil Mine."

Finding Sitka's map,
the girl was pleased as punch.
She guessed where Sitka'd gone.
Now to prove her hunch. . . .

Arctic Ocean

ALASKA

Bering Sea

Nome

Denali

Yukon River

Her journey wasn't easy—
the trail was mighty tough.
It seemed her luck was sour.
How did she cause this stuff?

Wild, windy williwaws,
short days with no sun,
mudflats and mosquitoes,
she made 'em, every one.

Fall, and still no Sitka.
Gold leaves fell off the birch.
Snow would soon shut down
Prickly's sister search.

Downcast, Prickly slumped,
feeling mighty slight.
Thinking of her sister,
she called into the night:

O-Yodel-lay-hee-hee...
Yodel-lay-tee-o

A team of wolverines
burst from the Northern Lights,
with Sitka driving hard—
what a skookum sight!

"Sis, where have you been?"
Prickly huffed at Sitka.
Sitka said, "C'mere, squirt.
Wow, I really missed ya!"

"My, you've grown," she marveled,
looking rather sad.
Prickly heaved a sigh.
"All I do goes bad."

"Now that we're together,
things will even out."
Sitka hugged her sister,
then began to shout:

Yodel-lay-tee-o

Yodel-lay-hee-hee...

The sisters teeter-tottered
on the crescent moon.
While critters shimmy-shimmied,
they belted out a tune.

"Yodel-lay-tee-o.
Yodel-lay-hee-hee.
If it weren't for the Rose girls,
what would Alaska be?

"No Denali and no Yukon,
no great salmon run—
moldy toes and mosquitoes
just add to the fun!"

When their song was over,
the girls began to doze.
Critters snuggled up
to the wild sisters Rose.

Being different as two flowers,
sometimes sisters disagree,
but the Roses loved each other
for all eternity.

For my bookends: Mom and Kye
—S. G.

For Barks, my little sister, the inspiring,
wild adventuress who does it all
—J. L.

Text copyright © 2014 by Shelley Gill
Illustrations copyright © 2014 by Judy Love
All rights reserved, including the right of reproduction
in whole or in part in any form. Charlesbridge and colophon
are registered trademarks of Charlesbridge Publishing, Inc.

Published by Charlesbridge
85 Main Street
Watertown, MA 02472
(617) 926-0329
www.charlesbridge.com

Library of Congress Cataloging-in-Publication Data
Gill, Shelley.
    Prickly Rose/Shelley Gill; illustrated by Judy Love.
       p. cm.
    Summary: A rhyming story about a girl named
Prickly Rose, who follows her ten-foot-tall sister
Sitka north, riding orcas and reshaping Alaska's
coasts and mountains.
    ISBN 978-1-57091-356-3 (reinforced for library use)
    ISBN 978-1-57091-357-0 (softcover)
    ISBN 978-1-60734-631-9 (ebook)
1. Tall tales. 2. Sisters—Juvenile fiction. 3. Adventure stories.
4. Stories in rhyme. 5. Alaska—Juvenile fiction. [1. Stories
in rhyme. 2. Adventure and adventurers—Fiction.
3. Sisters—Fiction. 4. Tall tales. 5. Alaska—Fiction.]
I. Love, Judy, ill. II. Title.

PZ8.3.G4216Pr 2014
813.54—dc23   2012039607

Printed in Singapore
(hc) 10 9 8 7 6 5 4 3 2 1
(sc) 10 9 8 7 6 5 4 3 2 1

Illustrations done on Strathmore Bristol
    vellum with transparent dyes

Display type set in Bonehead by CAKE Publications
Text type set in Chaparral Pro by Adobe Systems Incorporated
Color separations by KHL Chroma Graphics, Singapore
Printed and bound September 2013 by Imago in Singapore
Production supervision by Brian G. Walker
Designed by Diane M. Earley

Arctic Ocean

Alaska

Yukon River

Nome

Fairbanks

Ophir
Anvil Mine

Denali

Redoubt

Epicenter of the
Great Alaska Earthquake

Anchorage

Cook Inlet

Lituya Bay

Sitka

Bering Sea

N

0   100   200   300

Scale of Miles